Disney · PIXAR
INSIDE OUT

Sadly Ever After?

JOY

SADNESS

To Madeline,
whose endlessly
fascinating Mind World
dazzles me every day.
—Love, Mom

For my girls: Julie, Emma,
Libby, and Lolly.
—Dan

ISBN 978-0-545-93346-9

12 11 10 9 8 7 6 5 4 3 2 1   16 17 18 19 20 21

Printed in the U.S.A.   40

First Scholastic printing, January 2016

Disney·PIXAR
INSIDE OUT

Sadly Ever After?

by **Elise Allen**
illustrated by Daniel Holland

SCHOLASTIC INC.

This is Riley. Isn't she amazing? She lives in Minnesota and is great at doing lots of things—like skating. Look how fast she can go!

We did lots of things that day. We played Frisbee . . .

I feel **sad.** We wanted to take that dog home, but Mom and Dad wouldn't let us.

Um, okay . . . I guess I have no choice but to relive one of our most terrifying memories **ever**.

It makes me furious! That bus driver left three seconds early that day!

And we nearly choked to death on the bus exhaust! **So** beyond gross.

It was like being trapped in a horror movie! AND we were going to get in trouble for being late to school!

That's all very interesting. But do you want to know how *I* remember that day?

It was the
BEST
DAY
EVER!

Mom ended up driving us to school. We sang out loud to the radio and even stopped for hot chocolate! Don't you remember how amazing it was?

You're right, Joy. Maybe that wasn't so bad.

Who could be grossed out by hot chocolate?

I feel all warm and cozy and safe now.

That *is* a good memory, Joy. I feel . . .